This Little Tiger book
belongs to:

_____

_____

_____

For Charlotte, with all my love xx ~ T C

For my cousin Felicity ~ A E

LITTLE TIGER PRESS
1 The Coda Centre, 189 Munster Road,
London SW6 6AW
www.littletigerpress.com

First published in Great Britain 2012
This edition published 2013

Text copyright © Tracey Corderoy 2012
Illustrations copyright © Alison Edgson 2012
Tracey Corderoy and Alison Edgson have asserted their rights to be
identified as the author and illustrator of this work under the
Copyright, Designs and Patents Act, 1988

A CIP catalogue record for this book is
available from the British Library

Printed in China • LTP/1400/0526/1012

2 4 6 8 10 9 7 5 3 1

Just One More!

Tracey Corderoy   Alison Edgson

LITTLE TIGER PRESS
London

Teatime was over. Bath time was over.
That meant just one thing . . .
   "Story time!" cried Little Brown Bunny.
   So Mummy read him a story.
Then another. Then *another*!

"Just *one* more," begged Little
Brown Bunny.

So Daddy read him one more story, right to the end.

Still Bunny said, "Just one more?"

"Granny's turn!" cried Daddy Rabbit.

When Granny had read *all* the dragon books,

and Grandpa had read them *again*, Little Brown Bunny still wanted . . . "Just one more!"

Mummy Rabbit gave a great big yawn.

"But Little Brown Bunny, look!" she said. "We've read all your stories, see? No more stories means it's time for sleep."

"Oh," said Bunny.

"Maybe," he whispered,
"I'll *make* a bedtime book.
A super, super-long one!
Then story time will last
all night."

Next morning Bunny hopped out of bed.
  "Hooray!" he cried. "Time to make
my story."

He bounced across to his making-things box.
Soon he was writing big, long words and
drawing lots of pictures.

At last, he heaved up his heavy book.
This was going to be the longest
story *ever*!

"Are you sitting comfortably?"
he asked his toys. "We might be here
a long, long time!"

Two minutes later, it was all over.
"MU-U-UM!" called Bunny.
"My super-long story wasn't
super-long at all."

"Don't worry," said Mum. "Why don't you go and ask your friends what stories *they* like? Then you can add them to your book."

"Clever Mummy!" cried Little Brown Bunny, and off he went.

CARROT COTTAGE

Little Owl was playing with his rocket when Bunny bounced in.

"*My* favourite stories," he hooted, "are ones about the moooooon! One day I'm going to fly there! Zooooom!"

"I love the moon, too!" said Bunny.
"Thanks, Owl!"
    And he blasted off to find Little Mouse . . .

Little Mouse was having a teeny snack when Bunny bounded in. "I love stories about cheese!" she mumbled. "Big cheese, small cheese, round cheese, pongy cheese – *any* cheese really!"

"Thanks, Mouse!" giggled Bunny, holding his nose. And he raced off to find Little Wolf . . .

Little Wolf was having a tea party when Bunny came by.

"Well, I do love stories about piggies!" he said. "And that grandma with the big, furry ears!"

"*My* favourite story," grinned Big Daddy Wolf, "is the one all about . . ."

"Hugs!"

"Oh, Daddy," giggled Little Wolf, "what big *arms* you have!"

"All the better to hug you with!" chuckled Daddy Wolf. And he gave his boy a big daddy kiss on the nose.

"Thanks for your help," Bunny
called. Then he huffed and puffed
all the way back home!

Little Brown Bunny got out his book and scribbled down stories of moons made of cheese, and rockets and big, fluffy hugs.

By the time he had finished, it was dark outside.

"Come on, everyone!" he called. "This is going to be the best, most super-duper storybook *ever*!"

He opened it ever so
carefully and took a big,
deep breath. Then Little
Brown Bunny . . .

. . . fell fast asleep!

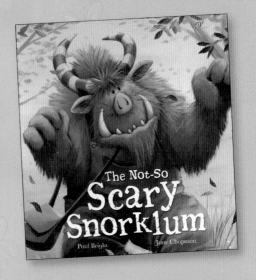

The Not-So
**Scary
Snorklum**

Paul Bright   Jane Chapman

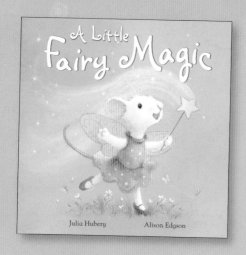

A Little
Fairy Magic

Julia Hubery   Alison Edgson

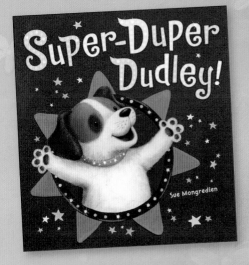

**Super-Duper
Dudley!**

Sue Mongredien

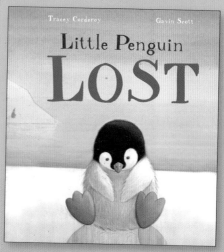

Tracey Corderoy   Gavin Scott

Little Penguin
LOST

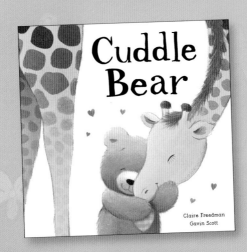

**Cuddle
Bear**

Claire Freedman
Gavin Scott

**The Little
White Owl**

Tracey Corderoy   Jane Chapman

Just ~~one~~ a few more fantastic book**s**

from Little Tiger Press!

For information regarding any of the above titles
or for our catalogue, please contact us:
Little Tiger Press, 1 The Coda Centre,
189 Munster Road, London SW6 6AW
Tel: 020 7385 6333 • Fax: 020 7385 7333
E-mail: info@littletiger.co.uk
www.littletigerpress.com